We Won the Lottery

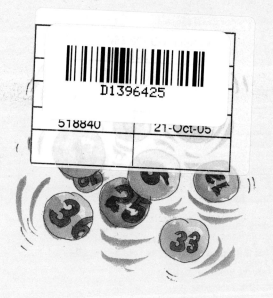

Shoo Rayner

Collins

Look out for more *Jumbo Jets* from Collins

First published by A & C Black Ltd in 1996
Published by Collins in 1997
12 11 10 9
Collins is an imprint of HarperCollins*Publishers* Ltd,
77–85 Fulham Palace Road, Hammersmith, London W6 8JB

The HarperCollins website address is
www.fireandwater.com

ISBN 0 00 675285-3

Copyright © Shoo Rayner 1996

The author and the illustrator assert the moral right to be
identified as the author and the illustrator of the work.
A CIP record for this title is available from the British Library.

Printed and bound in Great Britain by
Omnia Books Ltd, Glasgow

CHAPTER ONE
The Dreaming

Have you ever dreamed of winning the Lottery? Of course you have. I used to do it all the time.

Everyone in my family dreamed of winning the Lottery.

Dad wanted a new car.

My horrid sister, Clarissa, wanted Dig – Dig the pop star, that is. He's all she ever used to talk about.

Dig!

If I won the lottery I could have my own private concert.

As for my mum, she wanted to meet the Queen and have everyone call her Lady Jackson-Jones.

More than anything my mum wanted people to think she was really posh.

Mum tries so hard. She only buys tasteful things in our town, then she goes all the way to the next town (in the hope that no one will recognise her), to buy the embarrassing stuff like spot-cream, toilet paper and . . . Lottery tickets. She thinks that really posh people don't do the Lottery, so we try to keep it a big secret.

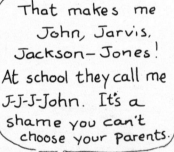

Mum's so stuck-up, that when she married Dad, she put her maiden name in front of his.

Jones is frightfully common. Jackson-Jones is so much better. It's double-barrelled, don't you know?

That makes me John, Jarvis, Jackson-Jones! At school they call me J-J-J-John. It's a shame you can't choose your parents.

My friend Kevin likes to wind Mum up. If he stays at our house for tea, he always covers his food in tomato ketchup and asks where the chips are. Mum hates it!

Mrs Jackson-Jones? This spaghetti has got leaves in it.

Tee-hee!

Those are herbs, Kevin. Don't you know anything?

Clarissa, my horrid sister, really really spoils Mum's attempts to be posh. Ever since she fell in love with Dig, she's been wearing strange clothes and has stopped brushing her hair completely.

My daughter??? Goodness, no! We're just looking after her for a friend.

CHAPTER TWO
Saturday Night

On Saturday nights we don't actually watch the Lottery but somehow the television always happens to be on.

Mum pretends to be writing out dinner party invitations, Dad pretends to be reading the paper, Clarissa pretends to be listening to her Walkman and I pretend to be doing my homework.

On our big night, the Lottery programme started as usual. A couple of winners got their cheques, a brass band played a tune and received a lot of money to buy new instruments, and a tiny village in Scotland was given money to build a new sports hall. Then it was time to concentrate on this week's numbers.

Welcome, it's a roll-over week and tonight's jackpot is estimated to be over twenty million pounds.

Mystic Maggie appeared, all dressed in black with moons and stars in her hair. She began making her predictions.

I turned bright red.

That's me!

Slowly . . . very slowly,
I lifted up my jumper.

I couldn't find a clean vest
this morning, so I borrowed one
of Clarissa's.

I'd never really believed in Mystic Maggie's predictions before, but this was uncanny. We were really excited, and for once, we stopped pretending we weren't watching the programme and gave it our full attention.

An old comedian I'd never heard of came on and told a few jokes . . .

. . . then he pressed the button to set the balls rolling.

We knew our numbers off by heart. They were all based on our birthdays.

The machine made its first choice.

Yes. Dad's age

Yes. Mum's age (she says)

Yes! My Birthday
We'd won £10

Yes! Clarissa's Birthday

Yes! Dad's Birthday

Yes! Mum's Birthday!!!!!

BINGO
by
JINGO!

WE'D WON!

We'd won the Lottery!

We didn't need to bother about the
bonus ball.

WE'D WON
THE LOTTERY!

CHAPTER THREE
We're in the money!

What do you do when you've won the Lottery? When you've danced and sung songs and hugged each other all you can? When you've even hugged your horrid sister? Yuk!

We won!

Hip-hip...

Hoooray!

We won!

How do you actually get the money?

Dad looked at the ticket.

Look, there's a phone number on the back.

Mum phoned the number.

Yes... yes... yes... yes...

They think that we're the only winner! They'll send someone round on Monday to confirm. They say we shouldn't tell anyone in the meantime.

But it was hard to keep quiet about winning the Lottery. Dad happened to mention it to his brother.

We...

... won...

And Clarissa happened to mention it to a friend that phoned.

17

And Mum thought she could trust her best friend.

And I might just have mentioned it to my friend Kevin.

It was a big mistake.

I never knew we had so many friends and relations. By Sunday afternoon they were all in our sitting-room.

No one actually mentioned the Lottery, but they all had the same greedy look in their eyes.

Eventually Dad had the brilliant idea of telling them we'd only got four numbers correct. They soon disappeared.

On Monday morning a lady from the
Lottery came to see us. She looked very
stern.

Hello, I'm Lolly Priceworth
from the Lottery. I'd like
to check the details
on your ticket please.

She noted down the numbers and asked
Mum where she'd bought the ticket.
Then she went out to her car and made a
call on her mobile phone.

When she came back her frown had gone and her face had split into a huge smile.

We looked at the piece of paper, open mouthed.

It was a 'roll-over week'!

£20,973,458 - 27p

We were in shock! But Lolly was very business-like and she soon began making plans.

Lolly got on the phone.

That was it. There was no way we'd ever get Clarissa to change her mind. It's amazing what money can buy.

The week went by and Saturday finally
came. A huge stretch limo came to take
us to the TV studios. It was great. It had a
satellite TV and video games, a drinks
cupboard, phone and a fax. The driver
even had a uniform with a hat.

You could tell the neighbours were well
impressed.

At the TV station we met Edwin Rich, the Lottery show presenter,

And Mystic Maggie,

The producer showed us where to stand when we were called on stage and then she showed us to our seats.

A man started telling jokes to get us all in a good mood. Then it was time for the show to begin. We waited nervously in our seats as the producer began to count down the seconds.

10 9 8 7 6 5 4 3 2 1

Suddenly the Lottery theme was blaring out and the show was live on air.

A tiny village in Cornwall received some money for a new arts centre and a tin whistle band played a tune before they got their cheque to buy new instruments. Then it was our turn. The drums began to roll.

Thrum- drum- diddle- drum- drum-

Last week was a roll-over week and there was only one winning ticket. Here to collect their cheque for £20,973,458·27p is... the Jackson-Jones family!

We were blinded by the lights that were focused on our seats. We staggered up to the stage and stood on our marks. We were all grinning like idiots! Mum pretended it was all a big surprise.

Then a screen behind us ripped in two and there stood Dig! Clarissa fainted.

There's not a lot you can do when someone gives you so much money.

We carried on grinning until it hurt.

By the time Clarissa came round Dig was long gone.

29

CHAPTER SIX
Shock Horror

We all slept late the next morning. The first inkling of what was to come came on the radio as Dad was shaving in the bathroom.

...The giant Lottery win couldn't have come at a better time for the father of the Jackson-Jones family who, it is rumoured, was to lose his job next week...

What?

Later that morning, Mum was watching telly in the kitchen when suddenly, her best friend appeared on the screen.

And when I switched on the lunchtime news programme there was my teacher.

As for Clarissa, she heard something rather unpleasant on her headphones.

We went to get the Sunday papers, to cheer ourselves up. It was a huge mistake. We were on the front page of every one. Almost anyone we had ever spoken to had sold their stories.

ENQUIRER

SHOCK HORROR
Snobby Mum

Sunday Rock

Lottery-winning daughter is stupid, pop music crazy has a head full of pink cotton wool and terrible spots says her frier

SUNDAY VACUUM
all the dirt and lots of sucking-up!

Useless Lottery-winning father had fourteen girlfriends before he got married. They say what they think of him inside.

YOUNG SUNDAY

Thicko Lottery-winning son is no good at school cheats at games

33

CHAPTER SEVEN
Getaway

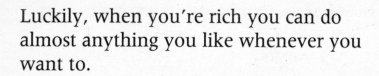

Luckily, when you're rich you can do almost anything you like whenever you want to.

So, on Monday morning we went down to the travel agents.

We want to get away quick. Somewhere where the sun shines and the sea is warm and blue.

I'll just check my computer... here we are. You can be breakfasting in paradise tomorrow morning.

Sounds great.

We rushed home, packed a few things, and phoned for a taxi to take us to the airport. Soon we were flying in a beautiful blue sky.

Before long we were settling into our sun-drenched tropical island total vacation location. We thought we were in paradise.

We weren't. We had the worst holiday
you can imagine.

We suffered from
sunburn

tummy bugs

creepy-crawlies

sharks

and
mosquitoes.

Worse still, someone recognised us from the papers . . .

. . . and soon Clarissa had loads of admirers who had found out how rich we were.

Dad spent all his time chasing them off.

On the way home, the plane was delayed for sixteen hours and we had to fly through a tropical storm. We looked pretty rough when we landed.

CHAPTER EIGHT
Welcome Home

We were really pleased to be back. It was cold, it was raining and there wasn't a shark in sight.

But when we got home, we could hardly get through the front door. The hallway was full of mail, and 99.9% of it was begging letters.

Dear Mr Jackson-Jones, please send us money. We n... of

Dear Jackson-Jones Family
    Congratulations on your fabulous
Lottery Jackpot win.
        In your hour of success, may
I draw your attention to our little
    charity that looks after
                    sick mice.

Dear Clarissa,
    have you ever thought about
all those poor rock-musicians
who need money to make
more music? Please give.

anks.

ots

ne

We got quite depressed reading all those letters. Most of them went in the bin, but there must have been at least three hundred that were really worthy causes. We put them in a box and promised to deal with them later.

What we needed was some advice. We telephoned Lolly Priceworth and she put us in touch with Mr Smiley, who was a financial adviser.

We took his advice, and after days trailing around huge mansions, we bought one of them, and Dad bought several large cars so that we could travel there in style.

It was the house of all our dreams.

I got a motorbike to ride around on and a
soundproof room of my
own with a mega-loud
CD system and
disco lights!

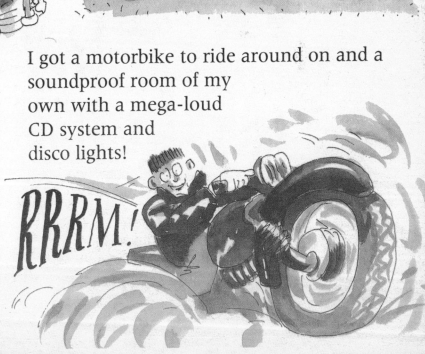

RRRM!

CHAPTER NINE
School

Now that we had a big, posh house and
drove around in big, posh cars, Mum said
I couldn't possibly go back to my nasty
old school, not after what my teacher
had said about me. So I was packed off to
St Toff's boarding school.

All the boys there
had noses that stuck
up in the air as
though there was
a bad smell
in the place.

All their mums and dads were either
Lords or Ladies, Sirs or Right
Honourables.

Of course, since I wasn't aristocratic, and
our family hadn't stolen all our money
from the peasants five hundred years ago,
I was treated as the school joke.

They gave me all sorts of nicknames but
as our money came from the Lottery, the
name Lotty stuck!

The food was terrible . . .

. . . we had
too much
homework . . .

. . . and at night,
I would lie in
my bed in the
dormitory, unable
to get to sleep.

CHAPTER TEN
The Summer Holidays

At last the end of term came, and our
new butler came to pick me up in a
Rolls-Royce.

Let me carry your bags
for you, young sir.

As well as a butler, Mum and Dad had got a cook. The food she made was awful, but I was not allowed to say so. She couldn't even make chips!

The cook and the butler were so snooty, they made Mum feel like dirt. When she asked them to do something they would say things like:

But Madam, we never did it like that when we were with Lord So & So.

Ah!

Mum took their word for it. She spent all her time tidying and cleaning and cooking and doing all the jobs that she wanted doing, while the cook and the butler sat around enjoying themselves!

My old friend Kevin came to stay for a few days but we didn't get on. He said that money had changed me.

During the summer holidays, we had a huge party for all our friends. But instead of being one big party, it ended up as four different parties. There were Mum and Dad's new rich friends in one corner . . .

. . . our old friends in another . . .

. . . our relations huddled in the kichen, moaning about how mean we were with our money . . .

. . . and Clarissa, who was having boyfriend trouble, dancing by herself to Dig's CDs . . .

It was a disaster. Our relatives started arguing about money and it wasn't long before the party ended up in a fight.

Mum and Dad's new friends walked out in disgust. So did the cook and butler.

The party was over in more ways than one.
Money had only brought us unhappiness.
We became lazy and forgot to tidy up and
empty the bins. The place went to rack
and ruin. So did Mum and Dad.

CHAPTER ELEVEN
Dawning

A while after the party, I was rooting around in the back of a cupboard, hoping to find something clean to wear, when I came across a cardboard box.

Inside were the begging letters that we received after our Lottery win. I started to read them. I was still there half an hour later when Dad found me.

What've you got there, son?

He read some of the letters.

We showed the letters to Mum and Clarissa. It didn't take long before we all came to our senses.

We had a family pow-wow and decided what we were going to do. We spent the rest of the day answering all the letters in the box and putting £1,000 cheques in each of the envelopes.

Then we sold the house . . .

. . . and the cars.

(Well, Dad was allowed to keep the Jag!)

And we bought our old house back.

We made sure that everyone was paid off and that we didn't owe anybody anything, then we looked at our bank account.

Because the money had been earning interest, we actually had more money now than we had won in the first place!

We chose our favourite charities.

Mum gave five
and a half million
to *Help the Children.*

Dad gave five
and a half million
to *Help the
Old People.*

Clarissa split five and a half million
between *Help the Whales* and *Help the
Rainforest.*

I gave five and a
half million to
Save the Animals.

That left five hundred thousand pounds.

We went to the bank and withdrew the money in cash. It filled two suitcases.

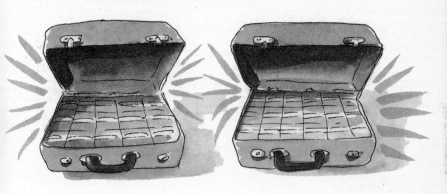

Then we phoned the TV station and told them to meet us on top of the tallest building in the country: The Universal Trade Tower.

We waited until the cameras were rolling,
then we threw the money to the four
winds.

There were cameras on the ground too.
That night, on the TV news, we watched
how the people down below had
scrabbled and fought as the money came
floating down from the sky.

I hope we made someone happy.

CHAPTER TWELVE
A Happy Ending

Mum's happy now. She doesn't feel she has to be posh any more.

Dad's still got his Jag which is all he ever really wanted.

And I'm back at my old school and best mates with Kevin again, like nothing had ever happened.

But Clarissa is the really happy one. She's got a new boyfriend who, she says, looks just like Dig. And she says he really loves her for herself.

He must do . . . who else would have her without a couple of million thrown in?!